MW00892343

This book belongs to

_____

George the Boss

Designed by Acorn Book Services. Publication Managed by Acorn Book Services
www.acornbooksesrvices.com * acornbookservices@gmail.com * 304-995-1295

ISBN-10: 0991368010
ISBN-13: 978-0-9913680-1-3

Illustrations by Vickie Froelich

George the Boss

by **C.S. McDonald**

Illustrated by Vickie Froelich

For Kiersten

This is George.

George lives at Pap-pap's
horse farm with his Thoroughbreds.

The horses love to stand under the shade
of the apple tree in the middle
of the pasture during the summer.

But George doesn't like all those big horses
taking up all his lovely shade. It is too crowded.
So he chases them away.

George will kick at the bigger horses...

George will nip at them, too!

The horses will stay away
from the shade
and George.

Because George
is the boss.

Kiersten loves to come to
Pap-pap's farm to ride George.
She always brings George an apple.

Pap-pap puts a saddle
and bridle on George.

And Pap-pap helps
Kiersten into the saddle.

But when Kiersten kicks George,
he plants his feet in the ground
and refuses to move!

Kiersten kicks and kicks and kicks. But George simply will not move. "Oh please, George, won't you trot for me? I brought you an apple!"

But George just stands there
refusing to budge!

Because George is the boss.

Soon the horses in the pasture won't play with George, because he won't share the shade of the apple tree with them.

George just stands under the shade all by himself, and watches Kiersten play with the kittens in Pap-pap's barn instead of riding him—
No apple today.

Because George is the boss.

Sometimes being the boss can be very lonely—
especially if you're a bossy boss.

One day Sally comes over
to stand in the shade of
the apple tree—
and George lets her.

And then the other
horses come to stand in
the shade,
and George lets them.
Hey, this is kind of cozy.

And then one day Kiersten comes to ride George.
She brings a nice big red apple.

Pap-pap puts on
George's bridle
and saddle...

Kiersten kicks,
and George takes a step.
Kiersten kicks again and
George takes another
step!

Soon George is trotting
all around
and the horses whinny
happily for George.

"I love you George!"
Kiersten says
as she hugs
him tightly.

George is no longer the boss...

But he sure is happy!

Made in the USA
Charleston, SC
25 August 2014